SUGAR HUBBY

BWWM BILLIONAIRE ROMANCE

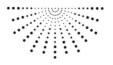

JAMILA JASPER

CHAPTER ONE

"Oh, God he's cute," I said, gazing at the photo on Zoe's phone, impressed by the masculinity I saw staring back from the screen. Dark skinned, black hair. A captivating gaze, seeming to look straight into my soul. He looked like a male model or something- not the type of person I could ever imagine landing myself.

"He is, isn't he?" said Zoe, almost glibly, like she didn't have any idea what an amazing catch she'd truly landed. "And shit, you should see the cock on him, it's *huge!* Do you want to? Let me find a photo. God, he gets so *deep...*"

I blinked at her for a moment, trying to understand the question. "What? No, no, no- that's really okay..." I said, my face heating up, and she gave me a smirk, like she was amused by my prudishness. "He does seem pretty great though. How long have you two been a thing?"

"Oh, we're not a thing," she said with a shrug, still swiping around on her phone.

"Oh?" I said, trying to make sense of this.

"I mean, *he* thinks we are. But right now I'm kind of just

playing the field. Exploring all my options, all that's out there..."

"Really?" I said, raising an eyebrow at her. "You don't feel bad about doing that? I mean if he thinks-"

"What? It's just *sex,*" she said, like it was the most obvious thing in the world to her, and it should be to me as well. "Why should a girl limit herself to just one dick? Guys sure as hell don't hold out on one girl, and you don't see them giving each other grief about it."

"Yeah, I... I guess so," I said, twitching my mouth to one side, doing my best not to make the comment on this subject that was circling around in my mind.

I'd been single for ages now, and honestly, I would have given anything to have a real connection with a man who looked as good as the one in the photo she'd just shown me. And I sure as hell wouldn't be running around with other guys if I found a man like that, either, risking it all for a sense of adventure.

But maybe I was just cut of a different cloth, and it wasn't my place to judge.

"Check him out," she said, showing me another photo of a man I personally found less attractive, but whose appeal to her I could see. Big, brawny, hipster bearded, slicked back haircut.

"Nice," I said, feigning enthusiasm.

"I have him over for booty calls whenever Devan is busy," said Zoe, turning the screen back to stare at her boy toy once more. "He is an *artist* with that tongue of his... I've got one hell of an arrangement going on."

"Yeah, seems like it," I said, taking an embarrassed sip of my coffee, and looking around the restaurant at other groups of friends and couples, all of them seeming far more at ease and in their natural element than I was at that moment.

"What about you?" Zoe suddenly asked.

"What about me?" I said, turning back to her, surprised.

Zoe smirked. "Who are you knocking boots with these days? Anyone special in your life?"

I'd really hoped that she wouldn't ask this. I always hoped that people wouldn't ask it, and yet they inevitably did. Like it was the most important thing they could possibly know about me.

"Oh, um... Well, no, not at the moment."

"What? Why not? A strong, sexy young black woman like yourself? I'd think you'd be getting laid every night of the week!"

I tried to think fast, looking away, and sincerely wishing that the two of us weren't having this conversation. "Oh, well, you know how it is. I'm trying to focus on my work at the moment."

This wasn't really true. I worked at a bookstore, and though I had aspirations of becoming a writer, I hadn't put out anything of merit whatsoever in quite some time.

"I mean sure, but a girl still has needs, doesn't she?" said Zoe, insistent.

"I mean, yeah, I guess," I said with a shrug. "But that's why a girl has a vibrator, right?"

Zoe grinned at me, and I sincerely hoped that this meant that my smutty answer satisfied her. The truth was, I had been single less from a desire to be single, and more from a sense of not knowing who I really was, or what I wanted from my life.

My life had taken an interesting course to the point where I was at now. My family had been very poor when I was growing up, but then my father got a steady, well-paying job around the time I started middle school, and that changed everything for me. I started going to a better school from that point onward, and found myself with new and better opportunities. I never quite seemed to fit in with

3

the other kids though, having been raised a certain way, gotten used to a certain set of norms, only to have it all thrown out the window when I was thrust into a wealthier crowd.

In any case, I gradually got used to things, and my life was on a pretty decent path until I started college. It was then, however, that my dad suddenly and unexpectedly lost his job, and I'd had to take out a huge student loan just to finish what I'd started.

So anyway, long story short, I now felt like I was living on the edge between two lives. Still associating with the people I'd met in high school and college, but not feeling like I related to them or understood them. They all seemed so shallow, so petty. They never seemed to have to worry about the same things that I did, but just to breeze through life like it was some walk in the park.

I'd become more and more withdrawn as time went by, so that now I really didn't do much more but go to work and then come straight home, not interested in dating or socializing, or doing any of the things that would supposedly help me find a partner.

I did get lonely sometimes- I wasn't going to deny that. But honestly, the struggle of meeting new people just didn't seem that worth it anymore. The annoyance of dealing with shallow pretty boys, or listening to gossiping girls telling me who I should sleep with and what I might be able to get out of them if I did. It all just felt like a headache, and one that seemed like it would take a lot more out of me than what I would be rewarded with in return.

"You know," said Zoe at last, with a note in her voice that suggested some mischief was afoot. "If you're single, there's a chance I might just know the perfect opportunity for you... How would you like to make an easy $50,000?"

I blinked at her, honestly not sure how to interpret this.

"Are you, like, a lady pimp now or something?" I asked her, and she laughed.

"You remember my brother, right? Max?"

I tensed up at the sound of his name.

Hell yes I remembered Max Saltzman, multi-millionaire editor of the fashion magazine *NY Look*. I'd only met him a couple of times, but it had been more than enough to make an impression on me- and not at all a favorable one.

Max was the kind of guy I thought of, in my private lexicon, as an *alpha-hole*- a sexy, confident, desirable man, an alpha male of alpha males, who also happened to be the very definition of a royal asshole. The sort of dude I might have conjured up in my sexual fantasies- and, if I was honest, I had done this a time or two- but who I couldn't even stand to be in the same room with in real life.

"Oh, Zoe, I don't-" I began to say, but Zoe held up her hands in protest.

"Now hold on, hear me out," she said. "Since Max started over at *NY Look*, he's kind of been giving people the impression that he's a family man- that he has a wife, he's trying for kids and all that. I guess the owners of the magazine are actually pretty old fashioned, and they wanted someone stable to make sure they weren't just going to have to sack him in a few months or whatever. But now there's this big New Year's Eve party coming up, and he's kind of backed himself into a corner. He can't show up without a wife or else he'll risk getting fired, and he's been looking pretty hard for someone to go with him-"

"And pretend to be his wife?" I said, somewhat shocked at the notion.

"Exactly!" Zoe said. "He's afraid if he asks someone he knows, someone from the party will recognize them and realize he's just making the whole thing up. Same with an escort- too much of a risk that someone there will have hired

5

them before or whatever... So really it would make the most sense if-"

"If he got someone who was dirt poor to go with him who nobody would recognize..." I finished for her.

"I was going to say, someone he could trust not to spill the beans. But I mean, it could be fun! Think about it! Hell, I would do it if I was in your situation! You get to spend the whole evening being arm candy at a fancy party with awesome food and top notch entertainment, rub elbows with New York's high society. Then go home fifty grand richer than you started out! Not a bad way to ring in the New Year, am I right?"

I gave her a deep frown. I really didn't think this was a good idea at all. I really didn't want to spend any more time with Zoe's brother than I had to, much less celebrate the New Year with him. I imagined him kissing me when the clock struck midnight, and found myself equal parts turned on and repulsed at the notion.

"God, I don't know... Let me think about it," I said, annoyed with myself for the certainty, even as I said the words, that the much needed offer of an easy fifty grand was going to prove far too sweet a temptation to resist...

CHAPTER TWO

He showed up at my door around 7:30. Dark brown hair. Piercing blue eyes. Flaring nostrils, a sexy goatee. A powerful body, which seemed to strain through his well tailored suit, leading my imagination into places where it really didn't want to go. And yet I couldn't stop myself from fantasizing, about coming back here at the end of the evening, letting him put those capable hands on me and unwrap the short little dress I was in, giving me the sweet, hard throttling of a lifetime...

"Is that what you're wearing?" was the first thing he said to me, instantly killing my lady boner, and making me incredibly self-conscious.

"What? What's wrong with it?" I asked, looking down at the tight, revealing thing, trying to see what he might be objecting to.

"Well, I mean your tits look great in it- real nice and perky. And that ass of yours won't quit! But I guess I was just hoping you'd come out in something a little more...fashion forward."

"Well I'm sorry, but this is the nicest dress I own," I said, already feeling like I had an idea of where this evening was going.

"Alright, alright, don't bite my head off," he said. "God, PMS much?"

I held my tongue, though just barely.

"Can we just go?"

"Wait, hang on," he said, and pulled out two jewelry boxes. "Let's doll you up a little bit. Maybe if you're shiny enough they won't pay any attention to what you're wearing."

Feeling sure now that this was a mistake, I was on the verge of becoming indignant at the prospect of letting him decide what I wore. I was seduced into complacency, however, when he looped a string of pearls around my neck, the smooth beads chilling against my clavicle, and every heated brush of his hands as they moved so delicately against my skin causing goosebumps to rise along my spine.

"God, they're beautiful," I said, turning to face myself in the mirror nearby.

"You aren't half bad yourself," he said, and I couldn't help but notice him staring at my ass in the mirror, clearly thinking I wouldn't see. I couldn't decide how I felt about this. "And here. If we're going to pretend we're married, you need to have a ring."

He took my palm in his own, and very gently slid a gold band onto my ring finger, the warmth of his fingers against the cool of the metal evoking a strange mix of sensations.

I experienced a rush of feeling, one which I couldn't quite explain.

"God, it's beautiful..."

"I'm gonna need it back after tonight," he said, "I borrowed it from someone. But the necklace you're free to keep."

Surprised by this, I fingered the pearls of the necklace,

wondering just how much the thing might happen to be worth.

Max stepped back, appraising me once more, and I smiled at him, hoping he might like what he saw.

"Damn. That's way better. You could almost be one of the girls in *NY Look!"*

"Really?" I asked.

"Well, almost."

My smile fell.

"Should we go?" I asked, really wanting to get this over this.

"Yeah, definitely! Unless..."

"What?"

"Well. You wouldn't maybe want to fool around a little before the party, would you, beautiful? That outfit is really doing it for me the longer I look at you..."

Jesus, what the hell was wrong with this man?

"What? No!"

"Why not?" he protested. "Jesus, you don't need to be all bitchy about it..."

"I have a boyfriend, okay?" I lied, hoping this might settle matters to at least some degree. "He's just out of town with family, and I agreed to do this as a favor to Zoe! That's all it is, alright? So just keep it in your pants and don't expect it to turn into anything more than what it is..."

"Christ, relax! I was just messing around, okay? Don't get your freaking panties in a knot..."

"Let's just go," I pleaded with him, and much to my surprise he actually agreed- holding the door open for me, and ushering me off, into what I was sure was bound to be a night to forget, if ever there was one...

3

CHAPTER THREE

Things didn't get any more promising from there. Max's car was nice, but he drove like a maniac, spending half the time gaping at his phone, and the other half tearing aggressively through the streets, honking at people to get the hell out of his way.

He cursed more than he spoke to me, and when he did speak to me, it was usually an attempt at flirting with me, of seducing me away from the boyfriend I'd invented.

"No one would ever have to know. I could do things to you that he wouldn't even think of..."

I was left squirming between desire and discomfort, and most of the time I simply resorted to gazing out the window, trying to ignore him, and wondering whether this humiliation was really worth the amount of money I was being paid.

At the end of the day, I had to concede that it was, but only just barely, and only because I was desperate...

Max was proving to be exactly what I'd pegged him to be—an *alpha-hole*. Capable of sweeping me off my feet at one moment, then driving me to my wit's end the very next. He acted so spoiled, so entitled. As if he somehow believed that the whole world belonged to him, and routinely got angry at it for refusing to recognize itself as his property.

The evening, of course, was just getting started at that point, and my already nasty impression of him only soured further once we made it to the party.

I don't think I'd ever felt as out of place before as I did that night among these people. Rich, pretty snobs, most of them looking so tightly wound that they might burst at any moment. With fake smiles, or more often than not, no smiles at all. The room emanated a sweltering sense of the innumerable power plays at hand. All the mingling and laughter was a cover-up for the exchange of social capital going on beneath the surface.

I sure as hell didn't enjoy hanging on the arm of my "husband," and being introduced to men who all ogled me relentlessly.

Max must have thought the same thing, as any time he wasn't using me as a prop to make him seem like the family man he claimed to be, he was busy checking out some twig fashion model, flirting shamelessly, evoking roars of laughter from whatever corner of the room he happened to be in.

I can't deny, as much as I'd been begrudging him up to that point in the evening, I began feeling quite jealous whenever I saw him with other women. Before leaving, I'd actually felt pretty good about myself looking in the mirror. Beautiful, sexy, confident. But then, once I was here, and once I saw him with all those other women, it drained away. Like, who the hell was I fooling? How on earth did I think I would fit in among a crowd like this, and why did I think any of this was a good idea?

"I need a drink," I muttered to myself, when I caught Max visibly peering down the dress of one of his groupies, wholly oblivious, it seemed, to my existence.

I had a few glasses of whatever the hell they were serving,

and managed to stop myself from getting too wasted, despite a burning desire to do just that. Then I made my way over to a table laden with cocktail shrimp, and decided that sounded like it would just about hit the spot at that moment.

I began stacking my plate with the things, when suddenly a shadow fell over me, making my skin crawl, and a nervousness overtaking me before I even knew exactly what was happening.

"Hey there baby," said a voice, and I held my breath, already wishing this situation would go away.

I turned very slowly, and saw a huge man in a suit looming over me, the type of idiot Max had been introducing me to all night, but not any specific idiot that I could immediately recognize.

I wanted to tell him that I wasn't his fucking baby, but instead I settled more diplomatically on a very tense, *"Hey..."*

"What's a pretty girl like you doing standing over here all alone? Why don't you and me go somewhere a little bit quieter, get better acquainted with one another? How does that sound?"

"No thank you," I said firmly, wishing I could get past him, but finding no opening to do so.

"Aw, why not? I like a little dark meat from time to time..."

He licked his lips at me, and I thought I might throw up.

"Please move," I said, trying to step forward, but the man was resolute.

"Aw, come on, don't be such a bitch! Come a little bit closer!"

Suddenly his hands were on me, his palms sliding down my abdomen, then rolling back and cupping my ass. He let out a nasty chuckle, and I started trying to slap his chest, wanting to dislodge myself, but not wanting this to escalate into violence on his part if I hit too hard.

12

"Stop it! Get off of me! Fuck off!"

"Marcel, what the hell?! Get the fuck away from her!"

A voice I hadn't been expecting boomed out suddenly, and I turned to see Max striding forward with sheer fury in his eyes, his nostrils flaring like those of a bull. The drunkard, evidently called Marcel, turned slowly, scowling at Max.

"For Christ's sake, Max, we're just having some fun! What do you care, you little sissy?"

"Get away from her," Max repeated, more sternly this time, as if to say he wasn't fucking around.

At last Marcel let go of me, and turned slowly to face Max, leaving my heart pounding as I watched the two of them- never in a million years would I have pictured Max standing up for me, but I found myself endlessly grateful for him having done so.

"God, she's just some fucking skank, Saltzman. Here spreading her legs to try to get ahead like all the rest of them. Why don't you piss off and go find a dick to suck?"

"Leave. Her. Alone."

Marcel glowered at him, growing angrier and angrier at Max's resistance.

"You aren't listening, are you?" said Marcel. "Well, then, maybe you'll hear this..."

Before I knew what was happening, Marcel's fist was in the air. I shrieked as it flew toward Max's face, and Max ducked at the last second, dodging the blow. Marcel roared, throwing his full weight at Max, and there was a sickening crack as the two of them collided. Marcel threw Max into a table and it collapsed beneath their collective weight, the entire party coming to a halt as the two of them tumbled around on the ground.

Marcel had had the element of surprised and the factor of his immense bulk on his side, but the better fighter soon revealed himself once the two of them were on equal footing.

The two men hit and kicked and did their damnedest to seize one another, but it was Max who finally crawled back up onto his feet, delivering a swift hard kick to Max's ribs, and standing over him victoriously, panting at the heap of a man lying at his feet.

At last, once it was clear that Marcel was down for the count, Max looked back up again, and stared into my eyes.

"Are you alright?" he asked, and it took me a moment to decide the answer to this.

My heart was beating like mad, and tears were streaming from my eyes- a fact I hadn't realized until now. I started shaking my head, feeling like I couldn't breathe, and just wanting to be away from there, as far from this party and from all the people around me as possible.

"No, no, I- I just want to go... Can I go home, now, please? I'm sorry..." My voice cracked as I spoke, and all I really wanted was to disappear.

"Yes, yes, of course. Of course we can go," said Max, a gentle hand suddenly pressed against my back, guiding me on with an assurance I hadn't previously imagined he could possessed.

The whole night felt ruined, and even though it wasn't, I felt as though it had all been entirely my fault...

CHAPTER FOUR

W e drove home in chilly silence, much slower this time than before. I stared out the window, gazing at the lights of the city, which didn't seem to evoke any feeling whatsoever from within me.

Before long, Max was walking me up to the door of my apartment, our footsteps incredibly loud as we moved along, an awkwardness swelling between us that began to feel unbearable.

"Listen," Max finally said, once we made it to the landing, and I looked him in the eyes, feeling hollow and empty. His face looked beautiful in the soft light of the city night, and I had to try and ignore this fact. "I'm sorry..."

"What? Don't be sorry. It wasn't your fault."

He shook his head, though.

"No, I mean... This whole evening... It was a really stupid idea. I shouldn't have dragged you into that mess. And I shouldn't have been treating you the way I was up to that point, either. I'm just used to it, I guess- that's kind of how everybody treats everybody in my line of work. Not that that's an excuse, obviously. But seeing that jackass, acting like it was- it felt like looking in a mirror, or something. I've spent so long trying to be just like assholes like him, to impress them. And honestly... I don't know what it is, but you seem a lot more like the kind of person I really would rather be like. You're so kind. So modest. So sweet."

I was honestly taken aback by this, not having expected to witness such a change.

"I mean," I said, "it really wasn't so bad up until that point. And I appreciate you stepping in for me like you did..."

"Yeah, well. I just hope it wasn't too awful for you. And I promise you, I will be adding another $25,000 to what I'm paying you for that whole fiasco. You shouldn't have been subjected to that..."

"Oh," I said, even more taken aback by this. I almost made the mistake of saying that wasn't necessary, but stopped myself, truly needing the money as I did, and not wanting to dispute the matter.

"I think it would be best if we both just try to forget about this. You should go in, get some rest. If you could just give me back that ring I'll get out of your hair. I'll get the money to you through Zoe, if that's alright."

"Oh, uh. Yeah. Yeah that would be alright," I said. As badly as I'd wanted the night to end up until now, I suddenly found myself dreading that very moment, wanting to delay it somehow. I reached for my "wedding ring," and began wiggling it down off my knuckle, the digit feeling naked as I pushed the gold band up to the tip of my finger.

And then, suddenly, before I had the chance to hand the thing over to him, we both jumped at the sound of an explosion in the distance.

We turned, and saw fireworks launching up from the skyline, painting the black sky with a shimmering rainbow of colors, and a chorus of voices ringing out in the distance through the cacophony of sound.

"It must be midnight," I observed quite obviously, and at once the two of us turned, and stared deep into one another's eyes. The moment seemed to go on forever, his clear blue irises drawing me in, his beautiful, angular face lighting up and darkening as the fireworks continued to go off in the distance.

I don't know just what came over me in that moment. All I know is that it did, and when it did, I found myself wholly powerless to resist it.

I leaned in, at the exact instant that Max was doing the same.

Our mouths met, and I savored the taste of his lips on mine. Warm. Soft. Sensual.

He pulled back on me, and I pulled on him in return.

We separated for an instant, taking in a single breath. We exchanged eye contact, and then we were right back on one another once again.

He slid his tongue into my mouth.

He pulled my body in close to his, and I wrapped my arms around his neck.

I felt him harden up against me, and I felt myself growing wetter and wetter with every touch, every caress, burning for him as the sky exploded overhead.

All of the sudden we were at the top of a rollercoaster, plunging straight down at a ninety degree angle, with nothing in the world to slow us down, or to stand in the way of our biologies' demand.

We burst through the door of my apartment, and found our way to my bedroom in no time.

He threw me against the wall, and we devoured one another, our hands sliding ravenously over each other's bodies, his lips on my neck, his teeth in my skin, and my entire being his, and happily so.

He had me out of my dress in no time, and I tore him out

of his shirt, loving it as he pulled me against his powerful chest in nothing but my bra and panties, my heaving stomach soft and delicate against his rugged, heaving abdominals.

"Fuck, I need you," I whispered into him, as he kissed me on the neck once again, then reached up, and seized my chest in his palms. He squeezed my breasts, and a surge of pleasure roared through me, my whole body aching for him, the room spinning around me as I melted in his grip.

I reached back in return, and held him through his pants. His cock felt magnificent in my fingers, long and hard and hot, and he shuddered as I rubbed it through the fabric, wholly unable and unwilling to resist my touch.

Unable to stand the separation a moment longer, I slid my body free of his grip and sunk down onto my knees in front of him. I jerked open the button of his pants and tore down the zipper, then almost violently slid his cock out into the open, savoring the heat of it directly against my had, loving his mild, masculine scent as I pushed the skin back, and a clear, thick drop of jizz formed on his swollen tip, leaving me no doubt whatsoever about the extent of his desire for me.

I pushed the skin forward again, pulled it back, and the fluid drizzled down along the course of his shaft, rolling between his testicles, leaving a clear, shining, and delectable trail for me to follow at will.

I brought my mouth just up to the tip of his cock, breathing steadily on him, loving the way he tensed up, and his nuts tightened up against his body in response to the warm air being pushed between my lips. Then I lowered my head, sticking out my tongue, and gently placing its tip against the seam of his scrotum.

I moved up slowly, licking clean the trail of his jizz, and loving his every response as I made my way up and up and up, his glorious muscles flexing and spasming with every move that I made. I took a deep breath and then held it, and slid my mouth forward around him, swallowing him nice and deep, gagging myself as the head of his cock touched down against the back of my throat.

"Oh, fuck," he sighed, and I pulled slowly back on him. Working my way back up, up, up to the head of his rock hard erection, holding my lips sealed around him, and then at last popping my mouth free- his shudder as I released him was the sweetest thing in the world to me at that moment.

I went down on him again. I swallowed him back up, and I began to pump my face along his body, in a slow, rhythmic motion. He ran his fingers through my hair, petting me sweetly as I sucked him off. Easing me further and further up into him, well beyond past what I was certain I could stand, but always releasing me at just the last second, showing me mercy, stirring up such incredible pleasure in me that I couldn't think of anywhere in the world I would rather be.

I loved the feeling of that cock throbbing in my mouth. I loved his grunts of pleasure, his moans of joy as I ran my tongue along his sack, making it so tight against that powerful body of his. I found myself craving him, wanting so badly for him to bust in my cheeks and fill my lips with his hot cum. I wanted to taste him, to swallow him. To let his scalding load drip across my tits, my belly, my thighs.

I wanted to feel claimed by him, possessed and fulfilled in the way that only he could. A man so powerful, so composed, so in control of the situation.

I didn't see him as an alpha-hole anymore- but instead, as a pure, unadulterated alpha male. The source of infinite pleasure. The only one in the world who could give me what I wanted.

And he did give me what I want- just not what I was expecting.

He shoved his cock up all the way into me, and held me against his body with his balls throbbing against my lips. He

JAMILA JASPER

groaned, and I felt certain I was about to taste the excess of him, spilling over into me, feeding my insatiable appetite.

Instead, he pulled out of me, still throbbing, his cock shining with spit, but his load still wholly intact.

He took me by the hands, and led me over to the bed with a sense of desperate urgency. I loved the way he handled me, commandeering yet gentle. Taking total charge, and letting me know exactly how badly he needed to get himself inside me.

He threw me down onto the bed and pulled my ass into the air, leaving me down on all fours with my face against the mattress, my heart racing, my head spinning as I anticipated the heat of his body inside mine.

He tore down my panties viciously, bringing them down around my knees, then he climbed up on me, mounting me, the wet heat of his shaft sending shivers along my spine, as he rested it against the crack of my ass.

He kissed the side of my neck, then slid his hands beneath the cups of my bras from behind, gripping them both fiercely, making me feel completely captive to him, as he positioned his body on top of my own, the tip of his cock resting against my tight, dripping pussy.

He pushed in hard, and he slid inside.

My eyes widened, and I tried to scream, but I couldn't make a sound.

Fuck, it felt amazing...

He stretched me out harder than I'd imagined as he shoved me full of his massive shaft, driving it up deep inside me, his tip careening into my g-spot with an unexpected force, and sending waves of pleasure echoing throughout my entire body.

This time I did scream.

"Fuck, you're wet, aren't you?" he said, easing his cock all the way in, savoring the heat of my body, his heart pounding against my shoulder as he held me there, in my own little slice of heaven.

He began to move inside me.

He pulled out, and then struck back down, even harder than before. My spine arched, and my fingers curled against the bed. He gripped my breasts more intensely, and I loved feeling so confined, his delectable mass bearing down on me from all angles.

His muscles slid along my spine as he fucked me. His hands pulled back against my chest, and tightened around me, so that no matter which way he moved it was like a knot, growing smaller and closer around me with every move he made, reducing me to less and less in his embrace, leaving me exactly where I wanted to be.

"Yes! Yes! Yes!" I begged him. "Please, fuck me! Please, please fuck me!"

His grunts of pleasure were unbearable as he hammered at my g-spot like a man on a mission. His thrusts growing harder and harder in response to my urgings. His sweat rolling along my spine. My pussy getting hotter and wetter, the muscles getting tighter and tighter around him, as if trying to clamp him so deep inside me, to sustain the pleasure forever.

The fireworks outside seemed to grow louder and louder as he loved and pounded and fucked me, drowning out the hammering of the bed against the wall, the vicious slapping of his drenched flesh against my own, the suction of our bodies as he entered and withdrew from me, and our vigorous screams of utmost pleasure, the ecstasy becoming so intense that I just couldn't stand it anymore.

Until finally Max roared, alpha male that he was, and threw the full force of himself up inside me. He slammed into my g-spot with the force of a meteor, my senses spiraling out of control as he gasped and came, shooting torrents of his thick, hot cum up inside me. He filled me almost instantly, shooting his load in deep and then pushing it hard back out of me in its abundance, spilling his sweet essence all over the bed, and an unbearable orgasm at last taking me over after what had begun to feel like a neverending buildup.

A crescendo of sensations tore through my body with a delirious force. Rushing up between my legs, radiating through my belly and out along my limbs, to the tips of my fingers and toes. The fine hairs on the back of my neck stood on end. My body tensed, and its delicate form pressed up against the mass of the man bearing down on me, the contrast delectable as he continued to pump himself full of me, holding me there through an endless climax, making me feel secure and fulfilled in a way that I had never really known before.

Then at last, almost at once, it all seemed to dissipate suddenly. I gasped, and nearly collapsed onto the bed as Max eased himself out of me, my body feeling empty after having been filled to such capacity, and my skin tingling all over as I lay there in the cool of the afterglow.

"God, what a way to ring in the New Year," he said with a gasp, looking as surprised as I was at what had just taken place. "Has anyone ever told you you're one hell of a wife?"

I laughed, and grabbed him by the neck. "Come here," I said, pulling down my bra, and pressing his face into my breast, his lips wrapping dutifully around my nipple, and the suction intense as he pulled back and suckled happily against my exhausted, sweat soaked flesh.

I had no idea where this all might lead from here, if anywhere. But that had just been the best sex that I had ever had in my life, and I couldn't think of a time when I had ever felt happier than I'd been wrapped in his arms, writhing with pleasure in his embrace.

I was more than happy to have been so wrong about this

incredible man, and whether or not things progressed from here, as I truly hoped that they would, he was spot on about one thing- this had been one hell of a way to ring in the new year...

THE END

AFTERWORD

Dear Reader,

Thank you so much for reading Book #2, *Sugar Hubby*.

For making it all the way to the end of this book, I want to offer you a **FREE gift**. 🎁

This offer is exclusively for readers:

Sign up to my newsletter and receive **3 FREE BWWM romance novels** just like this one, as well as a **FREE BWWM romance audiobook**.

If you LOVE reading romance and you want instant access to more FREE books, click the link below 👆.

Click here to sign up: http://bit.ly/jamilajasper

Enjoy the freebies!

Jamila

READ BOOK #3: KING SUGAR

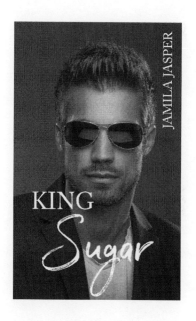

Click the picture above to read Book #3

FREE SAMPLE: FRENCH KISSED

CHAPTER ONE

Sitting with Earl meant forgoing relaxation. Since Lucy could remember, her father had always required proper etiquette, full engagement, and appropriate dress whenever he requested a meeting with one of his daughters. Lucy still felt a slight twinge of terror when she was meeting with her father, even if he had mellowed out over the years and she was certainly far stronger than him when it came to physical strength.

He'd ruled over his daughters with an iron fist and age couldn't change the fact that he was her daddy and daddy's word was law.

Lucy waited in the sitting room for her father to come out with "drinks" for the two of them. She wore a deep oxblood dress that highlighted the gorgeous undertones of her dark, mahogany-toned skin. Lucy's hair coiled densely on top of her head held together in a bun by a strained band. Her dress hit just below her knees and on her feet, she wore a pair of two-inch heels. Anything higher and not only would she tower over her father Earl, but he would be sure to give her a lecture about the impact of high heels on the balls of her feet. She wouldn't want it to affect her game now, would she?

Lucy could hear the blender stirring up a ruckus from the other room. Of course when Earl said "drinks" he meant a protein shake for Lucy and whiskey on the rocks for himself. Lucy would have rolled her eyes if it wasn't so entirely predictable of him. Lucy crossed her legs at the ankles and waited, silently glancing at her phone to see if her sister had called. There was nothing from her twin sister, Diana. Of course not. She knew better than to try to stick her head in on days when Lucy and Earl met up to talk tennis.

Earl finally entered with a frothy white protein shake for his daughter and a glass of whiskey for himself. He grunted as he squished into his chair, the impact of sitting down almost seemed to knock the wind out of him. Lucy noticed how much he'd slowed down over the past ten years. He'd aged faster since his wife had fallen sick…

"Here you go doll," Earl said, gesturing to the tray on the center table. Lucy grabbed the drink and clamped her lips down around the straw, leaving the light imprint of dark, plum lipstick.

"So… How are you doing papa," Lucy asked.

Earl smiled, "I'm good, doll but you know we ain't here to discuss how I'm doing."

Lucy nodded and sighed, "I know. It's about tennis."

"Recently, I've been watching your tapes and I just think something's off Lucy. Now... The tournament is soon and I just think you should talk to Milo and come up with something new. I'm paying him all this damned money for what?"

Lucy sighed. Having her father as her manager was both a blessing and a curse.

Lucy answered, "I'm fine dad. You don't have to worry, Milo's doing a good job."

Her coach Milo had been with her for the past five years and Lucy wasn't interested in finding a new one. Especially not so close to a tournament.

"I don't know if we should trust him..."

Lucy replied, "Well you say that about everyone and so far Milo has helped me win. A lot. You're too suspicious."

"Young lady..."

"I know, I know... I don't know what to tell you, dad. Milo looked at the tapes and he thinks I'm just tired. I need more rest."

Earl scoffed, "More rest?! You think you win so many matches because you spend valuable training time resting?"

Lucy knew there was absolutely no getting through to her father. She sipped on the remaining drops of her smoothie and sat quietly, waiting for him to continue speaking.

"Listen, child. I know you think I'm being a hardass for nothing but winning is how we keep your image good. Winning is how we get deals with Adidas or with Gatorade. You know they aren't exactly racing to you the way they are with Jenny."

Lucy cringed. Jennifer Winslow was her main tennis rival but she hadn't managed to beat Lucy once in the past eight years, even if she'd come close a couple of times and had given Lucy a run for her money. Despite her serious losing streak, Jenny had managed to sign deals with Lululemon, Powerade, Nike and more.

Both Lucy and her father knew the reason for that was the fact that Lucy was a black woman. Lucy could dominate on the courts but she had to work twice as hard to get half as much credit as a skinny blonde in the tennis world.

"I'm going to win. I need to win papa," Lucy said, reassuring her father that she was just as committed to the game as he was.

"I know you do, child. I'm just worried. I want you to be the best…"

"I know."

"Where's that sister of yours?" Earl grumbled.

Lucy smiled. Diana might have been right to stay away.

"I think she's out of town today," Lucy mumbled before trailing off.

Earl huffed and then twirled his mustache.

"She never comes to see me you know," He said.

Lucy knew that "never" was an exaggeration but she let Earl have his moment. Ever since his daughters had hit their thirties and spent weeks at a time away from him, he'd taken up exaggerating his loneliness to encourage them to visit more. Lucy was sure he'd made the same desperate plea to her twin sister Diana the last time she had visited.

Lucy's mood shifted as she thought about Diana and then her mother...

"No talking about mama I guess?"

Earl shook his head, "You ain't s'posed to worry about her 'til you're done that tournament."

"Y'all are too stubborn," Lucy muttered.

Earl smiled, "Damn right we are. Now, don't you have practice?"

Lucy rolled her eyes, "I think I can keep my schedule in mind on my own papa..."

"Why's your ass still sitting here, then? You need to be committed to winning Lucy. If I don't see some changes I'll get rid of that Milo fella..."

"Papa!"

"Don't chastise me, girl. Get down to practice so you can play better," He said gruffly.

Lucy brought her empty glass into the kitchen and then kissed her father good-bye. Sometimes his criticisms could be too harsh. He'd been managing his daughter since her tennis career began and sometimes the line between manager, coach and father blurred too much. When Earl finally retired from coaching Lucy directly, his grasp on her life had eased up a bit. But these days, Earl was finding creative ways to get an "in" to micromanage Lucy's tennis career.

She drove back home at the tennis court entrance of her house where Milo would be waiting. He was consistently ten minutes early and always carried on with Lucy about her chronic "lateness" which really meant being right on time.

As expected, Milo's Audi was already parked there. Years of high-level coaching meant Milo could afford more than a couple sports cars with six-figure price tags. Lucy wasn't impressed by it at all. She always thought guys who drove flashy cars tried way too hard.

"Lucy... You're late," Milo said as Lucy walked into her training room adjacent to the courts.

She ignored his comment and locked the door behind her. Lucy looked in the mirror at her shapely muscles and curves. After tennis practice, she'd need to hit the squat bar badly. Lucy knew that for most women, her strength would be a dream come true. But the truth was, having a body that looked nearly perfect meant hours and hours of training and sculpting. Sometimes the upkeep could get exhausting. One of the few things keeping Lucy going was the thought that she would be retiring soon. There was no way she would turn forty and still be playing this game...

Lucy changed into her tight white Nike skort that hugged the curves of her thighs and the shape of her thick ass. On her upper body, she squeezed her breasts into a custom-made sports bra. Lucy slipped into her tennis shoes and added a white headband to the entire outfit. She removed her piercings, makeup, and jewelry and then shoved them all into her gym bag. Now it would be time to face Milo's "wrath" at her lateness and hit as hard as she could. She needed to prove her father wrong. At the very least, that might earn her a real weekend off with no training for the first time in years...

She walked outside onto the court with her recently restrung tennis racquet. Milo was excellent at keeping her equipment in perfect working order.

"Ready to hit?"

Lucy nodded. When Milo started a workout nicely, she knew that she was in for trouble down the road. She took a deep breath and started their usual warm up. Today, Lucy's breath felt thick in her lungs. She knew that things had barely started but her mind was somewhere else, slowing her down. Keep this up any longer and she'd be forced to admit that her father was right about her training.

By the time Lucy was done with her workout, she was dripping with sweat. Her outfit still looked pristine and white as she walked to her cooler for a drink of water. Milo followed her with his hands on his hips.

"Lucy... That was awful," he chided.

Lucy glared at him as she wiped the sweat off her brow.

Lucy nodded, "Earl thinks so too. He took the time out of his day this morning to tell me he thinks I've been playing like garbage."

Milo grinned, "He doesn't mince words does he?"

🐚

Continue reading: My Book

READ "BLACK BRIDE, WHITE BALLER"

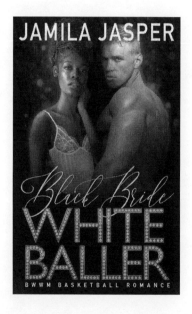

Click the picture above to learn more about my next romance novel.

MORE JAMILA JASPER ROMANCE

Keep reading past this section to find out how to get Jamila Jasper books for **FREE**!

FULL CATALOG BY JAMILA JASPER:

http://jamilajasperromance.com/2018/05/07/complete-amazon-back-catalog-jamila-jasper-bwwm-romance-author/

NON-EXCLUSIVE INTERRACIAL ROMANCE TITLES:

http://jamilajasperromance.com/2018/01/12/nook-kobo-ibooks-google-play-bwwm-book-list-published-wide-interracial-romance/

JAMILA JASPER ROMANCE AUDIOBOOK COLLECTION:

http://jamilajasperromance.com/2018/01/12/bwwm-romance-on-audio-book-jamila-jasper-interracial-romance-audio-collection/

PATREON

I've just launched a new opportunity for you to get a "backstage pass" to Jamila Jasper publishing by joining my Patreon!

For a small monthly fee, you get exclusive access to materials NOT available on my mailing list.

You'll receive:

Free short story audiobooks and audiobook samples when they're ready

#FirstDraftLeaks of Prologues and first chapters **weeks** before I hit publish

Notes from Jamila -- blog posts from my writing desk about my process so you can get to know the writer better

Click here to join: www.patreon.com/jamilajasper

Gold Subscribers, Platinum Subscribers, (and more) get

more exclusive content: you can get characters named after you, a mention in my dedication and even participate in deciding KEY aspects of the plot.

Check out the tiered subscription plans starting at $1.49/month, less than your daily morning coffee!

Click here: www.patreon.com/jamilajasper

SOCIAL MEDIA

Join me on social media! You'll find a reasonable number of daily posts, personal interaction & a welcoming community of interracial romance readers:

www.instagram.com/bwwmjamila
www.twitter.com/jamilajasper
www.facebook.com/bwwmjamila
jamilajasperromance@gmail.com
www.jamilajasperromance.com

ACKNOWLEDGMENTS

Thank you to my editor for your assistance and sometimes harsh critique in the production of this book. Thank you to @DeniaDesign on Twitter for your stunning cover design. Thank you to all the readers who enjoy pregnancy romance. I'd also like to thank all my social media followers for being a part of the Jamila Jasper family. Your support means the world to me. I'd also like to thank my local cafe for being the place where I get so much of my writing done each week!

5.99

61789834R00031

Made in the USA
Middletown, DE
20 August 2019